The Good Night, Sleep Tight Book

story and pictures by Mircea Vasiliu

gb GOLDEN PRESS • NEW YORK
Western Publishing Company, Inc.
Racine, Wisconsin

Good night,
   sweet dreams,
      I close my eyes
        and hug my pillow,

          Good night, good night,
          I'm asleep.

Sweet dreams!

My pillow floats,
cool and light,
like a cloud,

It takes me to
dream places...

tree places

sea places

sky places

high places

pillow places

my places !

We flew on our fluffy puffy dream pillows

WHOOPS!

I can stand on one seed

Watch out, here I come!

Here come my friends.
Hello, my friends.
How did you get here?
Did you float, too,
    on pillow clouds
        Like me?

Or did you walk
in your dream shoes?
Or maybe fly
with snowflake wings,
     or red balloons,
          or pumpkin seeds,
               or dragonflies?

Or . . . dragons!

Take me to my friend's house

Once upon
a time...

And another one   U P in a tree.

Sometimes I'm so small,
I crawl under a toadstool.

Nobody can find me there!

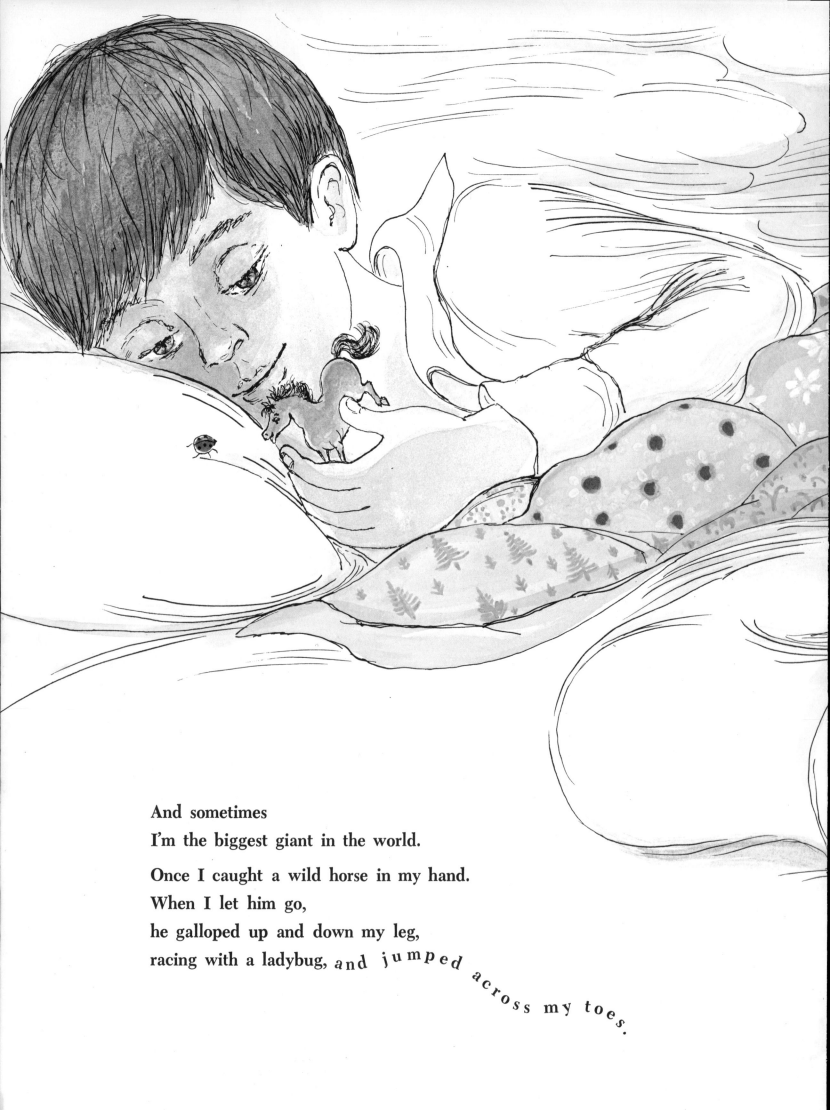

And sometimes
I'm the biggest giant in the world.

Once I caught a wild horse in my hand.
When I let him go,
he galloped up and down my leg,
racing with a ladybug, and jumped across my toes.

My elephant sleeps in a rose.

We go to see the King of Toys,
the Queen of Lollipops,
the fairy with the magic box,
the witch with toads and gingerbread,
the tiger in the turtle grass,
and the rabbit dancing with a tree.

Then we all go to see the Meadow Mouse.

We hop over roots and scramble through brambles.

Through the secret underground tunnel we TUMBLE.

We jump
and we s l i d e
till we come
to her underground
house.

We sail to sea palaces
and find
a mermaid and a sunken ship,

and two whales
in a peapod.

And all the
moonfish
and the
batfish
and the
cowfish
and a seahorse
come to see
a star
caught
in a pail
of water.
We listen to a fiddler crab.
We clap
and the candle flickers.
A puff of smoke says,
"Hush,
please let me sleep."

With my dream feet I can walk
up and down
and U P S I D E
D O W N
on the rainbow.

I can walk on my hands
and on my head
and I can talk upside down

and even

BACKWARDS.

COUNT A BILLION BUMBLEBEES

EIGHT — AT — 'TCHOO! — SEVEN — SIX — FIVE

A YELLOW TULIP FOR YOU AND A WOLLEY PILUT FOR YOU!

Would you like a slice of moon?

WHOOSH!

I can count from the end
to the beginning
and sneeze in the middle.
I can think a thousand thoughts
and say everything I like
and do anything I like.

We have a birthday party on a pirate ship
with funny hats and birthday cakes.
I blow a million candles out
and throw a million fireflies,
like fireworks,
against the sky.

Good night, good night,
I cuddle my pillow.
Sleep tight, sweet dreams,